Speeding Up, Slowing Down

by Natalie Hyde

🍄 Crabtree Publishing Company

www.crabtreebooks.com

Author
Natalie Hyde

Publishing plan research and development
Reagan Miller

Editor
Reagan Miller

Proofreader
Kathy Middleton

Notes for adults
Reagan Miller

Design
Samara Parent

Photo research
Katherine Berti
Reagan Miller

Prepress technician and production coordinator
Samara Parent

Print coordinator
Margaret Amy Salter

Photographs
Shutterstock: David Acosta Allely: pages 8 and 24 (bottom left)
Thinkstock: pages 1, 6 (top right), 7 (right), 15, 17
iStockphoto: page 19
Other images by Shutterstock

Library and Archives Canada Cataloguing in Publication

Hyde, Natalie, 1963-, author
    Speeding up, slowing down / Natalie Hyde.

(Motion close-up)
Includes index.
Issued in print and electronic formats.
ISBN 978-0-7787-0530-7 (bound).--ISBN 978-0-7787-0534-5 (pbk.).--
ISBN 978-1-4271-9019-2 (html).--ISBN 978-1-4271-9023-9 (pdf)

    1. Speed--Juvenile literature. I. Title.

QC137.52.H93 2014   j531'.112   C2014-900798-1
                                              C2014-900799-X

Library of Congress Cataloging-in-Publication Data

CIP available at the Library of Congress

Crabtree Publishing Company

www.crabtreebooks.com   1-800-387-7650

Printed in Canada/032014/BF20140212

Published in Canada
Crabtree Publishing
616 Welland Ave.
St. Catharines, Ontario
L2M 5V6

Published in the United States
Crabtree Publishing
PMB 59051
350 Fifth Avenue, 59th Floor
New York, New York 10118

Published in the United Kingdom
Crabtree Publishing
Maritime House
Basin Road North, Hove
BN41 1WR

Published in Australia
Crabtree Publishing
3 Charles Street
Coburg North
VIC 3058

Contents

In motion

When something is moving, it is in **motion**. Our world is full of things in motion. People swim. Marbles roll. Leaves fall. Motion is all around us!

Things cannot move on their own. They need a push or a pull to start moving. Pushes and pulls are **forces**. Forces create motion. Without forces, nothing would move.

5

Push and pull

A push is a force that moves something away from you. This boy uses a push to make his paper airplane fly away. A pull is a force that moves something closer to you. This girl and her father pull their suitcases behind them as they walk.

You use pushes and pulls every day. Your feet push against the ground when you walk, run, skip, or jump. You use a pull to lift a glass to your mouth to drink.

Keep a list of the pushes and pulls you use every day!

What is speed?

Speed is how fast something moves. Race cars move fast. They move a long distance in a short time. Distance is how far one place is from another.

Not all things move at the same speed. Many things move the same distance in different times. A turtle moves at a slow speed. You can walk around the block in less time than a turtle can! You move at a faster speed than a turtle.

Speeding up

The bigger the push or pull, the greater the change in motion. A big push or pull can make an object speed up, or move faster. Your feet push down and turn the pedals to make your bicycle move. To speed up, you must use a bigger push to turn the pedals faster.

What do you think?

If we added more dogs to pull the sled, would it make the sled speed up or slow down? Explain your thinking.

What is friction?

Friction is a force that makes things slow down or stop moving. When two objects rub together, friction is created. A soccer ball creates friction as it rolls on the grass. The friction makes the soccer ball slow down and then stop.

What do you think?

What happens when you touch the ground with your feet while swinging? Is this friction? How do you know?

More or less friction

Some objects create a lot of friction while others create less friction. The more friction an object creates, the greater the change in motion. A slide does not create a lot of friction. This girl moves quickly down the slide.

A bicycle's brakes use friction to help control the bike's speed. If you press gently on the brakes, the bike will slow down. If you press hard on the brakes, the bike will stop moving.

Smooth move!

Smooth surfaces create less friction than rough surfaces. A skateboard can move faster on smooth concrete than on a rough, bumpy road. A rough surface creates more friction that makes the skateboard slow down.

What do you think?

Will a toy car roll faster on a carpet or a hard floor? Explain your thinking.

Rough and smooth

The rougher the surface is, the more friction it creates. Sandpaper is very rough. You cannot slide on sandpaper. Plastic is smooth. This boy slides quickly on the plastic tube.

What do you **think?**

Gymnasts put chalk on their hands before they swing on the bars. Do you think chalk creates more or less friction?

Using friction?

To speed up, you need to make less friction. Skis create friction as they rub against the snow. Skiers put wax on the bottoms of their skis so there is less friction between the skis and snow. The wax helps skiers move faster.

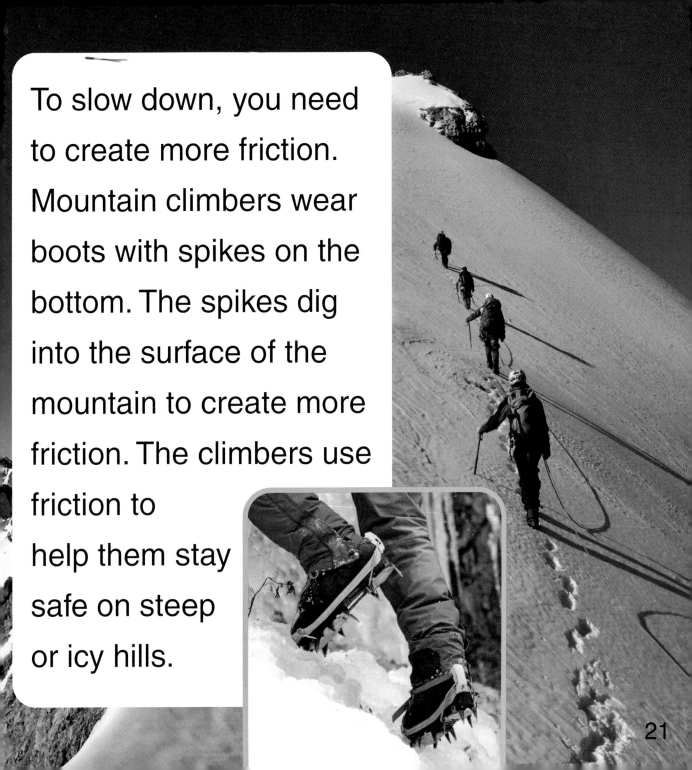

To slow down, you need to create more friction. Mountain climbers wear boots with spikes on the bottom. The spikes dig into the surface of the mountain to create more friction. The climbers use friction to help them stay safe on steep or icy hills.

Who needs friction?

Friction is an important force. Without it, things would never stop moving. The friction on the bottom of your shoes helps you walk without slipping and falling.

Without the friction from brakes, cars would crash into each other. Friction is a great help to us! Can you think of other ways we use friction?

Words to know and Index

forces 5, 12

friction 12,
13, 14, 15,
21, 22, 23

motion 4,
5, 10, 14

speed 8, 9,
10, 11, 15

Notes for adults and an activity

This activity gets children moving as they investigate how the strength of a push affects an object's speed.

Materials: Playground with a slide (a longer slide works best), a stopwatch, science journals or paper to record data, pencil, and masking tape
1. Use a piece of tape to mark a starting line at the top edge of the slide and a finish line at the bottom of the slide.
2. Introduce the purpose of the investigation as described above.
3. Demonstrate each of the three ways of sliding listed below. Demonstrate the timing process for children so the data is as accurate as possible.

Slide 1: No Push – Child sits at the top of the slide at the starting tape mark. The timer will say "1, 2, 3, Go!," The slider then leans slightly forward until gravity starts to pull him or her down the slide. The timer presses start as soon as the slider begins moving down the slide. The timer presses stop as soon as the slider crosses over the finish line.

The slider writes the time beside the corresponding slide type.

Slide 2: Self Push – The starting position is the same as above. When the timer says "1, 2, 3, Go!" the slider uses his or her hands to push off and start the sliding motion.

Time is again recorded as described above.

Slide 3: Partner Push – The starting position remains the same as above. A friend joins the slider on the slide. The friend stands behind the slider. When the timer says "1, 2, 3, Go!" the friend uses his or her hands to give a small push on the slider's back to help start the sliding motion.

Time is again recorded as described above.

Give children time to review their data and discuss the results as a class.

Learning more
Books
Move It! Motion, Forces and You by Adrienne Mason, Kids Can Press, 2005.
Why Do Moving Objects Slow Down?: A Look at Friction
    by Jennifer Boothroyd, Lerner Classroom, 2010.

Websites
Learn about the different kinds of friction with the Ducksters education website.
    www.ducksters.com/science/friction.php
This site examines different ways forces can change motion.
    http://eschooltoday.com/science/forces/introduction-to-forces.html